OFF
BASE

BY JAKE MADDOX

text by
Bryan Patrick Avery

STONE ARCH BOOKS
a capstone imprint

Published by Stone Arch Books, an imprint of Capstone.
1710 Roe Crest Drive
North Mankato, Minnesota 56003
capstonepub.com

Library of Congress Cataloging-in-Publication Data
Names: Maddox, Jake, author. | Avery, Bryan Patrick, author.
Title: Off base / Jake Maddox ; text by Bryan Patrick Avery.
Description: North Mankato, Minnesota : Stone Arch Books, an imprint of Capstone, [2022]
| Series: Jake Maddox JV mysteries | Audience: Ages 8-11. | Audience: Grades 4-6. |
Summary: Jayden is only one stolen base away from the school record when he is suddenly
kicked off the team, accused of cheating on a math test, and the "proof" is found in his
locker. Apparently someone is trying to prevent him from setting the record by framing
him, and he enlists the help of Lindsey, the school reporter, to gather clues and figure out
which of his teammates has it in for him—and do it before the final game.
Identifiers: LCCN 2021029854 (print) | LCCN 2021029855 (ebook) | ISBN 9781663974976
(hardcover) | ISBN 9781666329384 (paperback) | ISBN 9781666329391 (pdf)
Subjects: LCSH: Sports records—Juvenile fiction. | Cheating (Education)—Juvenile fiction.
| Baseball stories. | Friendship—Juvenile fiction. | Detective and mystery stories. | CYAC:
Sports records—Fiction. | Cheating—Fiction. | Baseball—Fiction. | Friendship—Fiction. |
Mystery and detective stories. | LCGFT: Detective and mystery fiction.
Classification: LCC PZ7.M25643 Od 2022 (print) | LCC PZ7.M25643 (ebook) |vDDC 813.6
[Fic]—dc23
LC record available at https://lccn.loc.gov/2021029854
LC ebook record available at https://lccn.loc.gov/2021029855

Designer: Heidi Thompson

Image Credits: Shutterstock: Suzanne Tucker, cover

Printed and bound in the USA.   4608

TABLE OF CONTENTS

CHAPTER 1
PRE-GAME.................................5

CHAPTER 2
BIG TROUBLE 13

CHAPTER 3
BLEACHERS.............................21

CHAPTER 4
QUESTIONS 29

CHAPTER 5
UNLIKELY PARTNERS 35

CHAPTER 6
CONFRONTATION.........................43

CHAPTER 7
PRACTICE...............................51

CHAPTER 8
SUSPECTS 57

CHAPTER 9
MORE QUESTIONS 63

CHAPTER 10
THE ANSWER............................71

CHAPTER 11
CONFESSION 77

CHAPTER 12
THE RECORD............................83

CHAPTER 1

PRE-GAME

Jayden Washington stood in the on-deck circle and looked up at the bleachers. A few students and parents had gathered. But Jayden knew that, soon, the bleachers would be packed.

The Roscoe C. Brown Redtails were two wins away from an undefeated season. Not only that, but Jayden was just one stolen base away from setting a new school record. The whole school had caught Redtails fever.

"Jayden!" Coach Anderson called. "Time for BP!"

Batting practice. Next to playing shortstop in the actual games, batting practice was Jayden's favorite part of playing baseball.

Jayden threw his bat over his shoulder and hustled to home plate. He stepped into the batter's box and took his stance.

"Ready!" he called.

Coach Anderson tossed the first pitch right down the middle. Jayden squared around to bunt. He always did that with the first batting practice pitch.

He laid the bat in front of the ball and pushed it down the first-base line. The ball rolled across the infield grass and stopped halfway toward first base.

"Nice bunt!" Cody yelled from the Redtails dugout. "That's an infield hit for sure."

Jayden looked into the dugout and gave Cody a thumbs-up. Cody was the Redtails starting center fielder and had given Jayden a few bunting tips during the season.

Coach Anderson threw a few more pitches. Jayden practiced pulling the ball into left field.

"Good job," Coach said. "Let's see you hit a few to right field."

Jayden opened his batting stance a little. Coach threw a ball over the outside corner of the plate. Jayden swung and hit a line drive down the right-field line. He hit a few more balls into right field before stepping out of the batter's box.

"All right," Coach called. "Who's next?"

Jayden walked back to the dugout and put his bat and helmet on the rack.

"Nice hitting," Cody said.

"Yeah," Abel said, "you almost looked like me up there."

Jayden laughed.

"Yeah, sure! Except I'm half your size, Abel," he joked.

They all laughed. Jayden and Cody had been friends since first grade. Abel and his family had emigrated from Mexico two years later, and the three boys had been best friends ever since.

Cody grabbed a bat and headed out of the dugout.

"I'm up next," he said. "I'd better get going."

Abel turned to Jayden and lowered his voice.

"How did the math test go?" he asked.

Jayden smiled.

"Great, thanks to you," he said. "Thanks for helping me study."

"No worries," Abel said. "Glad I could help. Now you can focus on making history today."

Jayden nodded.

"Which reminds me," he said. "Have you seen Nick? I want to ask him if I can keep the score sheet from the game. If I break the record, of course."

A tall boy with blond hair rushed into the dugout with a laptop under his arm. He wore a Redtails uniform with sneakers and no hat.

"Hey, Nick," Abel said. "We were just talking about you."

Nick froze.

"Why?" he asked.

"I was hoping I could keep the score sheet from today," Jayden explained. "If I break the record."

"Oh," Nick said. "I don't see why not." He set the laptop down on the bench.

"Want to see something cool?" he asked.

"Always," Abel said.

Nick smiled, showing off his teeth. Abel and Jayden could see Nick's braces, which were wrapped with red and gold rubber bands.

"Wow," Jayden said.

"I got them yesterday to match our uniforms," Nick said. "Team spirit!"

"Is that where you were yesterday?" Abel asked. "I wondered why you weren't at practice."

Nick nodded.

"I had to go to the orthodontist," he said. "One of my wires broke."

"Abel!" Coach called. "You're up."

Abel grabbed a helmet and a bat and walked out to home plate. Jayden grabbed a glove.

"I'd better go shag some balls," he said. He trotted out to the field.

Abel stepped into the batter's box and nodded at Coach Anderson.

Coach threw the first pitch. Abel swung and connected. The ball soared into center field toward Cody.

Cody didn't move. He just looked up and watched as the ball soared over the fence.

"Nice one," Jayden yelled. Abel performed a mock bow.

Coach Anderson started to throw another pitch but then stopped. A tall woman in a red dress came out of the dugout and walked out to the pitcher's mound.

What's Ms. Renner doing here? Jayden wondered. He felt a knot in his stomach. *Maybe I didn't do that well on the math test after all.*

Ms. Renner and Coach talked quietly for a moment. Jayden strained to hear what they were saying. Coach Anderson shook his head.

Then Coach and Ms. Renner turned and looked at Jayden. Coach Anderson pointed at Jayden and shouted, "Locker room! Now!"

CHAPTER 2

BIG TROUBLE

Jayden followed Coach Anderson and
Ms. Renner through the dugout and into the locker
room. They stopped in front of Jayden's locker, and
Coach Anderson turned to face Jayden.

"Before we go any further, is there anything you
want to tell us, Jayden?" Coach asked. "Now's your
chance."

Jayden looked from Coach Anderson to
Ms. Renner. She crossed her arms and didn't speak.

"Tell you about what?" Jayden asked.

"About your math test," Coach said.

Jayden's heart sank. *Did I fail after all?*

"I did my best," he said, shaking his head. "I really did. Abel and I studied for a week. I thought I did really well."

Ms. Renner sighed.

"You did do well," she said. "In fact, you got one of the highest scores in the class."

"Oh," Jayden said. "That's good, right?"

Ms. Renner shook her head.

"I have reason to believe you may have had some help," she said.

"Yeah, I did," Jayden replied. "I told you, Abel helped me."

Coach Anderson cleared his throat.

"Jayden, that's not what Ms. Renner means," he said.

"I don't know what you mean," Jayden said. "How else could I have done so well—"

He stopped talking as he realized what his teacher was saying.

"You think I cheated," Jayden said.

"Somebody stole a copy of the answer key to the test yesterday," Ms. Renner explained.

"It wasn't me!" Jayden insisted. "I would never cheat!"

"Not even if you needed to pass the test in order to stay on the team?" Ms. Renner asked.

Jayden plopped down on the bench in front of his locker.

"I would never cheat," he said again.

Coach Anderson sat down on the bench and put a hand on Jayden's shoulder.

"We all make mistakes sometimes," Coach said. "Better to admit it now so we can all move on."

Jayden shook his head and blinked away tears. He turned and looked at Coach Anderson.

"I can't believe you think I'd do this," he said. "I would never do something like that."

Coach grimaced.

"I didn't want to," he said. "But . . ."

"But what?" Jayden asked.

Coach Anderson looked at Ms. Renner.

"Someone saw you sneak into my classroom yesterday after practice," Ms. Renner said.

"No way!" Jayden said. He looked up at Ms. Renner. "Abel and I went straight home to study. I didn't go anywhere near the classroom."

"I would like to believe that," Ms. Renner said.

Coach Anderson stood up.

"Maybe we can put an end to this right here," he said. "We just need to look in your locker."

Jayden almost refused. But it wouldn't have mattered, he realized. School policy said they could search his locker at any time.

Besides, he told himself, *they won't find anything. I didn't steal the answer key.*

Jayden grabbed the lock and dialed the combination. Then he stood back.

Coach Anderson removed the lock and swung open the door.

Jayden could see his backpack, his lunch bag, and several bags of shredded bubble gum all piled up inside. Everything looked just as he had left it. Everything except the piece of paper sitting on top of the pile. It fell out of the locker and landed on the floor at Ms. Renner's feet.

She picked up the paper and held it out for Coach to see. A look of disappointment fell across Coach's face.

"What is that?" Jayden asked. He was afraid he already knew the answer.

Ms. Renner held up the paper.

"This," she said, "is the answer key you claim you didn't steal."

"I don't know how that got there," Jayden said. "I promise!"

Coach Anderson blew out a long breath.

"Jayden," he said, "sit down."

Jayden sat back down on the bench. *I can't believe this is happening,* he thought.

"Last chance," Coach said. "Did you steal the answer key to the test?"

Jayden shook his head. "I didn't," he said. "I promise."

Coach blew out another breath. "Okay then," he said. "Ms. Renner will need to take this to Principal Titus. I'm sure there will be more discussion tomorrow."

Jayden nodded.

"I understand," he said. "Can I go back to the field now?"

Coach Anderson shook his head.

"No," he said.

"No?"

"You can go out and watch from the bleachers," Coach said. "But you can't play."

Jayden felt his face get hot.

"I don't understand," he said. "I didn't cheat."

Coach Anderson pointed to the paper in Ms. Renner's hands.

"That paper from your locker says otherwise. Until we get this straightened out," Coach said, "you're off the team."

CHAPTER 3

BLEACHERS

Jayden took his time changing out of his uniform. He wasn't entirely sure he wanted to watch the game from the bleachers. But, after a lot of thought, he decided that he should go support his teammates, even if he couldn't play.

By the time he climbed up to the top row of the bleachers, the game was in the top of the third inning. The Redtails trailed 1–0. Their opponents, the Carson Cougars, where up at bat.

Malik, the Redtails starting pitcher, was on the mound. He walked the first batter on four pitches. As the batter jogged to first base, Malik walked around the mound and tried to regain his composure. He took a deep breath and stepped back onto the mound.

The next Cougars batter fouled off the first two pitches and was quickly in a hole.

Come on, Jayden thought. *Strike him out.*

Malik wound up and fired a fastball just off the plate. The batter swung, but the ball blew past him and smacked into the catcher's mitt.

"Strike three!" the umpire shouted. The crowd cheered.

"Yes!" Jayden yelled as he pumped his fist. "Great pitch!"

The Cougars catcher was up next. Runner on first, one out.

"Come on, Redtails!" Jayden yelled. "Double-play time!"

Malik wound up and delivered. The batter swung and hit a ground ball to the shortstop.

Double-play ball! Jayden thought.

Teddy, Jayden's replacement at shortstop, crouched down as the ball came toward him. He reached to his right, and the ball bounced up over his glove and rolled past him into left field. Abel raced in to get it, but by the time he got the ball, both runners were safe.

The crowd groaned.

Next up to bat was the Cougars first baseman. Jayden remembered that the first baseman was their best hitter.

Malik wound up and threw a fastball low and inside. The batter swung and drove the ball deep into left field.

Abel raced back toward the fence. At the warning track, Abel slowed and watched as the ball sailed over the fence for a home run. As the Cougars rounded the bases, Jayden looked up at the scoreboard. Cougars 4, Redtails 0. He sighed.

I can't watch, Jayden thought.

"Why aren't you playing?" he heard someone ask.

Jayden looked to his right and saw a girl he recognized sitting next to him. She wore a black baseball cap with a red *R* on it, and a matching messenger bag was slung over her shoulder. Jayden knew the *R* on the hat and the bag wasn't for "Redtails." It was for a college somewhere, but he couldn't remember which one.

"How long have you been sitting there?" Jayden asked.

"A while," the girl said. "You were really focused on the game, and I didn't want to interrupt." She stuck her hand out. "I'm Lindsey," she said. "Journalist for the *Redtail Reporter.*"

"That's right," Jayden said. "I thought you looked familiar. I'm—"

"Jayden Washington," Lindsey interrupted. "Star shortstop for the Roscoe C. Brown Redtails. Soon to be stolen-base record holder."

She pulled a small notebook and a pencil out of her bag.

"Which brings me back to my original question," she continued. "Why aren't you playing?"

Jayden looked at Lindsey's notebook.

"Is this an interview?" he asked.

"Of course," Lindsey said. "What journalist would pass up an opportunity like this?"

Jayden shook his head.

"It's complicated," he said.

He looked down at the field and watched as Malik walked another batter. The next batter hit Malik's fastball over the center-field fence for a home run.

Cougars 6, Redtails 0.

Jayden groaned.

Malik got the next batter to hit a ground ball to second base. Kevin fielded the ball cleanly and tossed it to first base for the third out. The inning was over at last. The Redtails hung their heads as they moved slowly toward the dugout.

Jayden jumped up and clapped.

"Come on, Redtails!" he yelled. "We can get back in this!"

Abel looked up at Jayden in the stands and mouthed, "What happened?"

"Later," Jayden mouthed back. Abel shook his head and jogged to the dugout.

Jayden turned and faced Lindsey.

"I don't want to be rude," he said. "But I don't really feel like talking about it."

Lindsey scribbled in her notebook.

"Does this have anything to do with why Ms. Renner came out on the field during warm-ups today?" she asked. "I assume that the math teacher doesn't normally show up at practice."

"You saw that?" Jayden asked.

"I see everything," Lindsey said. "That's what makes me a good journalist."

Jayden turned back toward the field.

"I don't want to talk about it," he said.

"What about the stolen-base record?" Lindsey asked. "Can we talk about that?"

"No."

Lindsey shrugged and stuffed her notebook back into her bag. She stood up.

"If you change your mind," she said, "come find me. I'm usually on the benches in front of the library or in the newspaper office."

Jayden watched her walk down the bleacher steps and then turned his attention back to the game.

Malik managed to keep the Cougars from scoring again, but the Redtails didn't have any luck at the plate. The Cougars closer struck out all three Redtails batters in the last inning to end the game. Final score: Cougars 6, Redtails 0. The Redtails' perfect season was over.

Jayden couldn't face his teammates, so he snuck out of the bleachers and walked toward the parking lot. His mom would be there soon to pick him up. His parents worked a lot and couldn't make it to many of Jayden's games. He was glad they weren't there today.

In the parking lot, he saw his mother's car parked at the curb and climbed in. His mother scowled at him.

"I got a call from your teacher today," she said.

CHAPTER 4

QUESTIONS

Jayden tossed and turned all night. He woke before sunrise and thought about what he should do next. The night before, he'd managed to convince his parents that he wasn't responsible for the stolen answer key. After that, he'd called Abel to explain what happened.

"Man, that's rough," Abel had said. "Don't worry, I'm with you. The whole team is with you. Redtails stick together."

Talking to Abel made Jayden feel a little better. It wasn't going to help him get back on the team, but it was a start.

What he needed to do, he realized, was figure out who put the test key in his locker. He went to school early to talk to the one person who might be able to help him.

He took a deep breath and knocked on the classroom door.

"Come in," Ms. Renner said.

Jayden pushed the door open and stuck his head in.

"It's me," he said. "Can I talk to you?"

"Jayden," Ms. Renner said with a smile, "please come in."

Jayden stood in front of Ms. Renner's desk.

"I promise, I didn't cheat," he said. "You have to believe me."

Ms. Renner stared up at Jayden for a few moments. She sighed, then nodded.

"I really hope that's true," she said. "I know you've had your struggles, but I've enjoyed having you in my class."

"It's true," Jayden said.

"Can you explain how the test key got into your locker?" Ms. Renner asked.

"Not yet," Jayden admitted. "That's why I came to see you."

"I don't understand," Ms. Renner said.

"You said yesterday that you heard from someone that I cheated," Jayden said. "I wanted to know who."

Ms. Renner shifted in her chair. "I see," she said.

Jayden waited. Ms. Renner turned and looked out the window.

"Ms. Renner?" Jayden said.

She turned and looked at Jayden.

"I can't tell you that," she said.

"But what if they're lying?" Jayden asked. "What if they cheated and put the test key in my locker to frame me?"

"I don't think he's lying," Ms. Renner said. "I don't think he'd have any reason to cheat."

"Okay, well, maybe he made a mistake then," Jayden said.

Ms. Renner shook her head.

"I'm sorry," she said. "I really can't help you."

Jayden walked to the door. He stopped and turned back to face his teacher.

"I'm not a cheater," he said.

Ms. Renner nodded.

"I want to believe you," she said. "I'll tell you what. I'll talk to Principal Titus and see if I can give you a makeup test."

"Really?" Jayden said. "That would be great."

"I'll get it arranged, and you can take it next week," she said.

"Next week?" Jayden said. "But the season will be over."

"I'm sorry," Ms. Renner said. "That's probably the best I can do."

"Okay," Jayden said with a nod. "Thanks."

Jayden closed the door on his way out of the classroom. He wandered down the hallway, weaving his way through the crowd of students arriving for school.

Next week is too late, he thought. *I have to figure this out now if I want to play on Friday.*

To do that, Jayden knew he would need some help. He turned around and rushed toward the library.

He found Lindsey sitting on a bench in front of the library entrance.

Lindsey was hunched over, scribbling in her little notebook. She didn't notice Jayden until he spoke.

"Uh, Lindsey?" Jayden said.

Lindsey stopped writing and looked up.

"Change your mind about that interview?" she asked.

"Not exactly," Jayden said. "The thing is, I came to ask for your help."

CHAPTER 5

UNLIKELY PARTNERS

Lindsey frowned.

"You need my help?" she asked.

Jayden waited for a group of students to pass before he answered.

"I'm in trouble," he said. "Big trouble."

Lindsey flipped to a blank page in her notebook and wrote "Jayden: Big Trouble" across the top of the page.

"Go on," she said.

"No way," Jayden said. "You can't tell anyone about this."

"I'm a journalist," Lindsey said. "Telling people stuff is kind of what I do."

"Not this," Jayden said.

Lindsey looked at her watch and stuffed the notebook into her bag. She stood up and started to walk away.

"I need to get going then," she said. "I'd be happy to help you with . . . whatever, but you've got to give me an interview."

She turned away.

"Wait!" Jayden said. "You'll help me if I give you an interview?"

Lindsey turned around and looked Jayden in the eye.

"I promise," she said.

The bell rang.

"I've got to get going," Lindsey said. "Meet me here at lunch and we'll get started."

"Okay," Jayden said. "Lunch."

The morning crept by as Jayden struggled to focus in class. He could only think about finding out who put that test key in his locker so that he could clear his name and rejoin the team.

When the lunch bell rang, Jayden raced to the library. He found Lindsay sitting on the same bench as before, eating a peanut butter and jelly sandwich. Jayden sat down next to her and pulled a turkey and Swiss sandwich out of his lunch bag.

"Where do I start?" he asked as he took a bite.

Lindsey pulled out her notebook and set her sandwich aside.

"Let's start with why you didn't play in the game yesterday," she suggested.

"I got kicked off the team," Jayden said. He was shocked at how quickly it came out.

Lindsey stared at him.

"Really?" she said. "I knew something big must have happened, but I had no idea it was this big."

"Well, now you know," Jayden said.

Lindsey closed her notebook.

"What happened?" she asked.

Jayden looked around to make sure no one could hear them talking.

"Ms. Renner thinks I cheated on a math test," he said.

"Why would she think that?" Lindsey asked. "Wait! You didn't, did you?"

Jayden shook his head.

"Of course not," he said.

"Then why?" she asked.

"That's why I need your help," Jayden explained. "Somebody told her I cheated. They also put a stolen answer key in my locker."

"Oh, that's bad," Lindsey said. "But how am I supposed to help?"

"You said you see everything," Jayden said. "Maybe you saw who Ms. Renner talked to after school yesterday?"

Lindsey took off her hat and put it back on. She picked up her notebook and flipped through the pages and then stared up at the sky as she thought.

"Yesterday after school?" she asked.

Jayden nodded. Lindsey smiled and jumped up from the bench.

"Come on," she said, "I might have something that could help you."

Jayden followed Lindsey through the halls to the student newspaper office. A hand-drawn sign announced: *"Redtail Reporter*: See your school from a *news* view."* Lindsey noticed Jayden reading the sign and shook her head.

"I know," she said. "It's silly."

Lindsey tapped on the door as she opened it and peeked inside.

"Good," she said. "Nobody's here."

She pushed the door open, and Jayden followed her inside.

Jayden looked around the room. It was smaller

than a typical classroom but still had several rows of desks. A large table stood at the front of the room. Piles of papers covered the desks and the table. Lindsey crouched down in the corner over a plastic bag. Jayden could see the bag was filled with trash.

"What are you doing?" he asked.

Lindsey kept digging through the bag and didn't answer.

"Lindsey?"

"Found it!" she said. She held a small slip of paper over her head.

Jayden reached for the paper, and Lindsey pulled it away.

"You promise I get an interview?" she asked.

"I promise," Jayden said. "What is it?"

"I collect the trash from the school office once in a while," Lindsey explained. "You know, for journalism purposes."

Jayden looked at the stack of trash bags in the corner.

"How often is 'once in a while'?" he asked.

Lindsey grinned. "Every day."

She held up the slip of paper.

"This is a note from Ms. Renner to the office, dated yesterday," Lindsey said. "Ms. Renner asked to have a certain student sent to her classroom after school."

"What student?" Jayden asked.

Lindsey squinted at the paper.

"Nick Something," she said. "I can't read the last name."

"Reilly?" Jayden asked.

"Yeah, that could be it," Lindsey said. "Do you know him?"

"Yes," Jayden said with a sigh. "He's our team statistician."

CHAPTER 6

CONFRONTATION

Jayden had to wait until after school to confront Nick. He found Nick in the Redtails dugout entering statistics into his laptop.

Nick smiled when he saw Jayden.

"Hey, Jayden," he said. "What are you doing here? Is Coach letting you come back?"

I wish, Jayden thought.

He looked out at the field. The Redtails were practicing fielding. The outfielders and infielders had split off into groups. Abel was hitting pop flies to the outfielders. Luis, the Redtails catcher, hit ground balls to the infielders. Teddy had taken Jayden's spot at shortstop.

"Unfortunately, I'm not here for practice," Jayden said. He sat down on the bench next to Nick. "I came to talk to you."

Nick tapped away on his keyboard.

"I'm a little busy," Nick said. "Maybe we can talk later."

"This will be quick," Jayden said. "I just want to know why you told Ms. Renner I cheated on the math test."

Nick stopped typing.

"What do you mean?" he asked.

"You went to talk to Ms. Renner in her classroom after school yesterday," Jayden said. "Whatever you told her made her think I cheated. I want to know what you said."

Nick looked at Jayden and shook his head.

"I don't know who told you that," he said.

"So, it's not true?" Jayden asked.

"Does that sound like something I would do?" Nick countered. "Why would I tell her something like that?"

"That's what I want to know," Jayden said.

Nick went back to typing. "I'm telling you, I wasn't in Ms. Renner's classroom. I can't help you," he said. "Sorry."

Jayden watched as Luis sent a ground ball toward Teddy. Teddy reached out for it, but the ball bounced off his glove and rolled into left field.

"Sorry!" Teddy called as he ran to retrieve the ball.

Jayden turned back to Nick. "You really didn't get called to Ms. Renner's classroom yesterday?"

Nick closed his laptop and looked at Jayden. "No," he said, "I didn't."

"You sure about that?" a voice asked.

Jayden and Nick both turned and saw Lindsey standing in the dugout.

"What are you doing here?" Jayden asked.

"I'm helping," Lindsey said.

She held up a slip of paper for Nick to see. "Isn't this a note asking for you to go see Ms. Renner after school?"

Nick frowned. "Where did you get that?" he asked, reaching for the paper.

"I'm a journalist," Lindsey said. She kept a hold of the note. "I don't reveal my sources."

"Okay, fine," Nick said. "I went to Ms. Renner's classroom, but I didn't tell her you cheated."

"What did you say?" Jayden asked.

"I just told her what I saw," Nick explained. "I saw you go into the classroom after practice the day before the test."

"But you didn't!" Jayden insisted. "I did not go into her classroom after practice."

"Yes, you did, Jayden" Nick said. "I'm sorry, but I saw you."

Jayden looked at Lindsey. He hoped she had

something to ask, because he was out of ideas. Lindsey was staring out at the field.

"There are no numbers on your practice uniforms," she said.

"No," Jayden agreed, "there aren't. What are you getting at?"

Lindsey sat on the bench next to Nick.

"How did you know it was Jayden if his number wasn't on his uniform?" she asked. "What, exactly, did you see?"

Nick thought for a moment.

"I saw Jayden down at the end of the hall near Ms. Renner's classroom," he explained. "He opened the door and went inside."

"Did you see his face?" Lindsey asked.

Nick shook his head.

"No," he said, "but I'm sure it was him. At least, I thought it was him."

"But he was far away, right?" Lindsey said. "And you didn't see his face?"

"Look," Nick said, "I'm pretty sure it was Jayden. But no, I guess I didn't see his face."

"Great," Lindsey said. She stood up and started to leave the dugout. "Thanks."

"Hold on a sec," Jayden said.

Lindsey grabbed Jayden's arm and pulled him out of the dugout.

"Where are we going?" Jayden asked as he followed her away from the field.

"Don't you see?" Lindsey asked.

Jayden thought about it. He shook his head.

"See what?" he asked.

"Nick thinks he saw you go into Ms. Renner's classroom," Lindsey explained.

"But I didn't," Jayden said.

"Right," Lindsey agreed. "But someone did. Someone in a baseball uniform."

"Oh," Jayden said. "So he saw one of my teammates."

Lindsey nodded.

"Someone on the team stole the answer key," Jayden said.

"And hid it in your locker," Lindsey added.

One of my teammates got me kicked off the team, Jayden thought. His stomach started to hurt.

CHAPTER 7

PRACTICE

Jayden turned to leave the baseball field and ran right into Coach Anderson. Coach smiled and clapped Jayden on the shoulder.

"I'm glad you're here," Coach said. "I wanted to talk to you."

Lindsey slung her bag over her shoulder and straightened her hat.

"I should get going," she said to Jayden. "We'll catch up later."

"Listen," Coach said, "I know you, and I don't think you're a cheater. But we have rules. That's why I couldn't let you play."

"I know," Jayden said.

"Still, there's nothing that says you can't practice with the team," Coach said. "Maybe you could suit up. It might take your mind off things."

It didn't take long for Jayden to get his practice uniform on and return to the field. The infielders were still doing fielding drills. Coach hit a ground ball to Teddy at shortstop. Teddy lunged toward the ball and missed badly. He ended up sprawled out on the infield dirt, and the ball bounced into left field.

Jayden trotted out to short and helped Teddy up.

"You're back!" Teddy said. "I'll get out of the way."

"Teddy, wait," Jayden said. "I just want to show you something."

Jayden stood next to Teddy and faced home plate. Coach hit a bouncing ball to short. Jayden sidestepped to his left and crouched in front of the approaching ball. He caught the ball and tossed it to Wyatt at first base.

Jayden turned to Teddy.

"It's easier if you get your body in front of the ball," he explained. "Then you don't have to reach for it. Even if the ball takes a bad hop, your body can block it. Give it a try."

Teddy stepped forward. Coach hit a grounder toward him. Teddy stepped in front of the ball and crouched with his glove in front of him. The ball hit something in the dirt and bounced up over Teddy's glove.

The ball hit Teddy in the chest and dropped to the dirt in front of him. Teddy scooped it up and threw to first.

"Nice job!" Jayden said. Jayden noticed Ms. Renner standing in the dugout. Coach Anderson noticed too.

"Jayden," he said, "come hit grounders."

Jayden jogged to home plate. Coach handed him the bat and walked to the dugout. Jayden grabbed a ball from a bucket next to the plate and looked at third base.

"Coming your way, Mason!" he shouted.

He hit a high bouncing ball down the third-base line. Mason raced forward toward the ball, grabbed it barehanded between bounces, and tossed it to first. Wyatt stretched out to make the catch at first.

"This one's yours, Teddy!" Jayden called.

He hit a hard grounder just to the left of second base. Teddy raced over and got in front of the ball. He fielded it cleanly and made the throw to first base.

"Nice job, Teddy!" Jayden said. He picked another ball out of the bucket.

"One second, Jayden," Coach Anderson said. He walked out of the dugout and back to home plate. He took the bat and ball from Jayden.

"Ms. Renner needs to speak to you," he said.

"That doesn't sound good," Jayden said.

Coach frowned.

"Go see what she has to say," he said.

Jayden trudged to the dugout. "Coach said you wanted to talk to me?" he said.

Ms. Renner nodded.

"I spoke to Principal Titus," she said. "She agreed that I can give you a makeup test."

"That's great!" Jayden said. "I won't let you down."

He thought about the sour look on Coach Anderson's face. Ms. Renner didn't look very happy either.

"What's wrong?" Jayden asked.

"I tried to work it out so that you could take the test tomorrow," Ms. Renner said.

"So, I could play in the game tomorrow afternoon?" Jayden asked.

Ms. Renner held up her hand.

"I said I tried," she said. "Principal Titus said no. She wants to sit in on the test, and she can't do it until next week. I'm afraid you won't be allowed to play tomorrow."

Jayden's heart sank.

"I'm sorry," Ms. Renner said. "I really am."

Jayden looked out at the field. His teammates had started doing sliding drills. One by one, each player ran from first base and slid into second base feet-first or headfirst. It was one of Jayden's favorite drills. He wouldn't be doing it again this season. His season was over, one stolen base short of the record.

"If I could prove I didn't cheat, would I be able to play tomorrow?" Jayden asked.

"I don't see why not," Ms. Renner said. "Of course, Coach Anderson would have to agree as well."

Jayden watched his teammates racing from first to second.

Is one of them really responsible for this? he wondered.

"Can you tell Coach I had to go?" he asked.

"Where are you going?" Ms. Renner asked.

"If I'm going to figure out who stole that test key," Jayden said, "I'm going to need some help."

CHAPTER 8

SUSPECTS

Jayden found Lindsey in the newspaper office. She sat alone, legs crossed, on the floor in the middle of the room. She stopped scribbling in her notebook and looked up when Jayden came in.

"Shouldn't you be at practice?" Lindsey asked, frowning.

"I was," Jayden said. "Ms. Renner showed up at practice and said that she could give me a makeup test."

"That's good," Lindsey said. "So, you'll be able to play tomorrow?"

Jayden shook his head and sat down next to Lindsey. "She can't give me the test until next week," he said.

"Oh," Lindsey said. "So, that's it? Your season is over?"

Jayden shrugged. "Probably so," he admitted. "The only way I'll get to play is if I figure out who stole the test key before tomorrow afternoon."

Lindsey made a face.

"That's going to be tough," she said.

"I know," Jayden said. "I was hoping you could maybe help me?"

Lindsey grinned and handed Jayden her notebook. He looked at the page and saw it was a list of all the members of the Redtails baseball team. Lindsey had drawn a line through Jayden's name.

"What is this?" Jayden asked.

"Our suspect list," Lindsey replied. "I've crossed

you off for obvious reasons. Is there anyone else we can cross off the list?"

Jayden read through the list and handed the notebook back to Lindsey.

"You can cross off Abel and Cody," he said. "They're my best friends. There's no way they would do this."

Lindsey's eyebrows rose slightly. "Are you sure?"

Jayden nodded. "I'm positive."

Lindsey crossed Abel and Cody off the list.

"Anybody else?" she asked.

Jayden thought for a moment. He shook his head.

"I don't know," he said. "I can't believe anybody on the team did this."

Lindsey tapped her pencil on the notebook and sighed.

"This is still a long list," she said. "Maybe we should look at this a different way. Who would benefit from you getting in trouble for cheating?" She circled a name on her list and showed it to Jayden.

"Teddy?" Jayden said. "I don't think so."

"How can you be sure?" Lindsey asked. "Why wouldn't he?"

"Well, because . . . ," Jayden trailed off. He didn't really have a good answer. Teddy was getting to play more without Jayden on the team. Could he really have done this?

"Look," Lindsey said, "I know these are your teammates, but they can't all be your best friends, right? And, if what Nick says is true, somebody on your team did this."

Jayden took the notebook from Lindsey and looked at the list again. He knew she was right. His teammates weren't all friends. And whoever stole the answer key was probably on that list. He circled two more names and handed the list back to Lindsey.

"Now we're talking!" Lindsey said. "Why these two?"

"Last week, Malik started complaining that I was getting too much attention for stealing bases when he was winning all the games with his pitching," Jayden explained.

"What about Wyatt?"

"We used to be really close," Jayden said. "Then Abel moved here."

Lindsey waited for him to say more. He didn't.

"And then?" she prompted.

"He said some things," Jayden said. "About Abel and his family. We stopped being friends that day. It was years ago, but we haven't gotten along since then."

"Oh." Lindsey stared at the list. "Is there anybody else?" she asked.

Jayden shook his head.

"I don't think so," he said. "Also, Teddy, Malik, and Wyatt are the only Redtails in Ms. Renner's math class. Besides Nick and me, of course."

Lindsey checked her watch and jumped up. She grabbed her bag and stuffed the notebook inside.

"I have to get going," she said. "Let's meet here before school, and we can go interview our suspects."

Jayden had an idea.

"Nick should be in the computer room before school," he said. "Let's ask him if any of these guys could be who he saw going into Ms. Renner's classroom."

"Good idea," Lindsey said. "That might help narrow down our suspect list."

Jayden followed Lindsey out of the newspaper office. As Lindsey walked away, Jayden could hear sound coming from the baseball field. He considered going back to practice but decided against it.

Could one of my teammates really have done this? Jayden wondered. He had less than twenty-four hours to find out.

CHAPTER 9

MORE QUESTIONS

Jayden and Lindsey met at the newspaper office in the morning and went to find Nick. Nick wasn't in the computer lab.

"What now?" Lindsey asked.

"We have thirty minutes until school starts," Jayden said. "Let's track down our suspects."

"Who should we start with?" asked Lindsey.

Jayden thought for a moment. "Let's go find Malik," he said. "He should be out on the baseball field."

They found Malik sitting cross-legged on the pitcher's mound with his eyes closed.

"What's he doing?" Lindsey asked.

"Visualization," Jayden said. "The morning of every game, he likes to come out here and imagine how the game will play out."

"The whole game?" Lindsey asked.

Jayden nodded and motioned for Lindsey to follow him. They walked out through the dugout and onto the field. They stopped near the pitcher's mound. Malik showed no sign of hearing them.

Jayden cleared his throat. After a few seconds, Malik opened his eyes and looked at Jayden. Then he turned his head toward Lindsey.

"You're that reporter, right?" he said. "No interviews."

"Actually, we're here because I need your help," Jayden said.

Malik grunted. "Make it quick," he said. "I need to finish up before school starts."

"I'm trying to figure out who stole the answer key from Ms. Renner," Jayden explained. "Or else I can't play today."

"And that matters to me because?" Malik asked.

"Come on," Lindsey said, "Jayden's one of your best players."

"We'll do just fine with Teddy at short," Malik said.

"What about the record?" Lindsey asked.

Malik stood up and stretched. He shook his head.

"The only record that matters to me is wins and losses," he said. "Jayden knows that."

"Did you steal the answer key?" Jayden asked.

Malik laughed.

"Is that what you think?" he asked. "No way. I couldn't have gone to the classroom after practice anyway. I stayed behind with Coach Anderson and worked on my slider. By the time we finished, the school was locked."

"Besides," he added, "I don't care about your record, but I wouldn't try to stop you from breaking it."

"Can you think of anybody who would?" Jayden asked.

"I don't know," Malik said. "But I'd bet it's someone who doesn't like you very much."

Jayden looked at Lindsey and mouthed, "Wyatt." Malik sat back down on the mound and closed his eyes.

Jayden and Lindsey walked across the field back to the dugout.

"Where can we find Wyatt?" Lindsey asked.

"He usually reads in the library before school," Jayden said.

They found Wyatt sitting at a table near the back of the library reading a graphic novel. Wyatt put the book down and frowned at Jayden.

"What?" he said blankly.

"Can we talk?" Jayden asked.

"Sure. Talk," Wyatt said.

"This will just take a minute," Jayden said.

"Let me guess," Wyatt said. "You're trying to

figure out who put the answer key in your locker, and you think it's me."

"Did you?" Jayden asked.

Wyatt stared at Jayden for a long time. His ears turned red.

"You really do hate me," he said. "All this time, I thought maybe we'd be friends again someday. But you really do think I'm an awful person."

Jayden didn't know what to say.

Finally, he spoke. "The things you said—"

"I was stupid. I didn't mean any of it," Wyatt said. "I was just mad you were spending so much time with Abel. But that was years ago. How can you still hate me?"

Jayden sat down. "I don't hate you," he said quietly. "I was just really hurt."

Wyatt took a deep breath.

"I'm sorry," he said. "For everything."

Jayden and Lindsey looked at each other.

"You mean it was you?" Lindsey asked.

Wyatt shook his head.

"I didn't steal the answer key," he said. "But I'm sorry for what I said about Abel, and I'm sorry this happened to you. I was rooting for you to break the record."

"Thanks, Wyatt. I appreciate it," Jayden said.

He stood up and extended his hand to Wyatt. Wyatt shook it.

"Let's go," Jayden said to Lindsey.

Outside the library, Lindsey turned to Jayden.

"Are you sure it's not him?" she asked. "He didn't really give us an alibi."

"It could be him," Jayden admitted. "But I really don't think he did it."

"That just leaves one suspect," Lindsey said.

Jayden nodded and looked at the crowd of students roaming the school.

"Teddy," he said. "But he'll be hard to find in this crowd."

The school bell rang.

"There's no time to look now," Lindsey said. "We can meet up at lunch to look for him."

"Maybe not," Jayden said. He pointed over Lindsey's shoulder. Teddy was walking toward them.

"Hey, Jayden," Teddy said. "Thanks again for the tips yesterday."

"No problem," Jayden said.

Teddy looked around, then lowered his voice.

"Are they going to let you play today?" he asked.

"I don't know," Jayden said. "Not unless I figure out who stole that answer key and put it in my locker."

"It wasn't me," Teddy said.

"With Jayden off the team," Lindsey said, "you get to start at shortstop."

Teddy rolled his eyes.

"I don't care about that," he said. "You've seen me play. I'm not very good."

"So, you didn't do it?" Jayden asked.

Teddy shook his head.

"There was no time. We had a family dinner

right after practice," he said. "Timmy and I left in our uniforms. We didn't even go back to the locker room."

The school bell rang a second time.

"I'm going to be late," Teddy said, and he rushed away.

"So are we," Lindsey said. "Let's meet up at lunch and figure out what to do next."

"Listen," Jayden said. "Thanks for helping with this, but we're out of suspects. Maybe it's time to give up."

CHAPTER 10

THE ANSWER

Jayden spent his morning classes thinking about who might have put the answer key in his locker. When lunchtime came, he was no closer to finding an answer. He went looking for Lindsey.

He found her in the newspaper office eating her lunch at the large table in the front of the room. Several students were in the office eating lunch or working on stories for the paper. Lindsey smiled when she saw Jayden.

"Did you come up with something?" she asked.

Jayden shook his head. "Nothing," he said. "And time is just about up."

Jayden sat down.

"I still owe you an interview, though," he said. "Is this a good time?"

"Oh," Lindsey said, "I guess I figured you wouldn't want to do it."

"I promised," Jayden said. "Remember?"

Lindsey dug her notebook out of her bag. She flipped to a blank page and grabbed a pencil off the desk.

"Okay," she said. "First question: What's it like to steal a base?"

Jayden grinned.

"It's my favorite part of the game," he said. "It's just me against the pitcher and the catcher. I have to figure out when to steal and when to stay."

"How do you know?" Lindsey asked.

"I just feel it," Jayden said. "There's a rhythm to the

game. My instincts take over, and I just sort of know when to run."

Lindsey scribbled furiously in her notebook. She hesitated before asking the next question.

"You tied the school record for the most stolen bases in a season," she said. "How did that feel?"

Jayden sighed.

"It's okay if you don't want to answer," Lindsey said.

Jayden shook his head.

"It felt pretty great," he said. "I guess I've been so focused on breaking the record, I'd forgotten that.

"My parents were there," he continued. "They both work a lot, so they don't make it to many of my games. Plus, Coach Anderson was there. It was his record I tied. It's a day I'll remember forever."

"You tied Coach Anderson's record?" Lindsey asked. "I didn't realize that."

"Coach went to school here," Jayden said. "Long ago, of course."

"Jayden, you don't think—"

Jayden's eyes widened. He shook his head.

"No way," he said. "Coach would never do something like that."

Lindsey shrugged.

"If you say so," she said. "But somebody did."

Lindsey asked a few more questions about Jayden's favorite baseball player, his favorite team, and what sport he'd play if he didn't play baseball.

They finished the interview just as the bell rang.

"Thanks for the interview," Lindsey said. "I'm sorry we couldn't figure out who put the answer key in your locker."

"Don't worry about it," Jayden told her. "Thanks for trying. I'll see you around."

Jayden hurried off to class. The rest of the day seemed to take forever.

When the final bell rang, Jayden threw his backpack over his shoulder and went to go watch the Redtails' final game. He had one stop to make first.

He knocked on the door of Ms. Renner's classroom.

"Jayden," Ms. Renner said, "come in."

"I can't stay," Jayden said. "I'm on my way to watch the game."

"It's nice that you're still going to support the team," Ms. Renner said. "In spite of everything."

Jayden nodded.

"They're still my teammates," he said. *Even if one of them tried to frame me,* he thought.

Jayden stared out the window and watched the students outside. Then he turned to face Ms. Renner.

"I never said thank you," he said. "For offering to give me the makeup test. You didn't have to do it."

"You don't have to thank me," Ms. Renner replied. "This whole incident has been a bit . . . unsettling. Besides, I believe in second chances. I don't know if we'll ever get to the bottom of this, but if you say you didn't do it, I'll give you the benefit of the doubt."

"Well, thanks," Jayden said.

"I do feel bad that it will keep you off the team," Ms. Renner said. "But we did find the answer key in your locker."

"I know," Jayden said.

Ms. Renner looked up at the clock.

"We should get going," she said. "The game will be starting soon."

Ms. Renner opened her desk drawer, pulled out a red and gold headband, and put it on.

Jayden stared at his teacher with his mouth open.

Ms. Renner laughed. "What?" she said. "Team spirit!"

Lindsey came rushing into the classroom. Jayden turned to look at her.

"I know who did it!" they both said.

CHAPTER 11

CONFESSION

Jayden raced to the baseball field, with Lindsey and Ms. Renner following close behind. They got to the field just as the Redtails finished batting practice. The Redtails gathered in the dugout while their opponents, the Brighton Buffaloes, took their turn warming up.

Jayden, Lindsey, and Ms. Renner burst into the dugout. Coach Anderson looked up from his clipboard.

"Jayden," he said, "what's going on?"

Jayden looked around the dugout. His teammates stared back at him.

"I figured out who stole the answer key and put it in my locker," Jayden said.

Cody stood up. "You don't think it was one of us?" he asked.

Jayden nodded. "It was," he said. "I didn't want to believe it either."

Coach Anderson looked at Ms. Renner. "Do you know what's going on?" he asked.

"No idea," Ms. Renner said.

"Ms. Renner, what time was the answer key stolen?" Jayden asked.

"I'm not sure exactly," Ms. Renner admitted. "Based on what I've been told, probably right after practice on Tuesday."

"Based on what you've been told?" Jayden asked.

"Well, yes," Ms. Renner said. "As you know, someone came forward with information."

"So, if they hadn't come forward, you wouldn't know when the answer key was stolen," Jayden said.

"No," Ms. Renner agreed. "I guess not."

"So, it might have been stolen earlier in the day?" Jayden asked.

Ms. Renner thought for a moment, then nodded.

"Yes, I suppose so," she said.

Jayden walked over and stood in front of Nick. Nick tapped at the keys on his laptop. Jayden looked back at Ms. Renner.

"You thought I stole the test because someone told you they saw me go into your classroom after baseball practice," Jayden said.

"Yes," Ms. Renner said.

"What if I told you that person wasn't here after practice?" Jayden asked. "In fact, he wasn't at practice at all that day."

Nick stopped typing and looked up at Jayden.

"What are you talking about?" Nick asked.

Lindsey stepped forward and handed Nick a piece

of paper. Nick looked down at the paper and turned pale.

"I saw Ms. Renner put on that red and gold headband, and it reminded me of the rubber bands you had on your braces," Jayden said. "You left school early on Tuesday to go to the orthodontist. That's a message from the office saying so."

With a sigh, Nick closed his laptop. He looked all around as if he were trying to figure out if he could run. Finally, his shoulders slumped and he handed the note back to Lindsey.

"I'm sorry," he said. "I didn't mean for this to happen."

Nick turned to Ms. Renner. "Jayden's right," he said. "I didn't see him go into your classroom after practice. I wasn't even here."

"Why did you frame Jayden?" Lindsey asked.

"I didn't plan to," Nick said. "I've had a hard time keeping up with my schoolwork since I became the statistician for the team. My grades have been slipping. I went to see Ms. Renner at lunchtime that day to ask for help."

Nick looked at Ms. Renner.

"You weren't there," he said. "But there were copies of the answer key for the test on your desk. I grabbed one and left. I didn't think you would notice."

"So, when I asked you about it," Ms. Renner said, "you knew I had noticed."

Nick nodded.

"So, I lied," he said. "I said I saw Jayden go in after practice, then I stuffed the test through the vents in his locker. I'm really sorry."

Ms. Renner looked at Nick and sighed.

"Well, Jayden," she said, "it looks like you've proved your innocence."

"Does that mean I can play today?" Jayden asked.

Everyone looked at Coach Anderson.

"Let's hope you can get your uniform on as fast as you run the bases," he said.

CHAPTER 12

THE RECORD

Jayden made it back to the dugout just as the game was about to start. The crowd cheered as the Redtails jogged out and took their places on the field. Jayden took his usual spot at shortstop. He looked up at the bleachers. It seemed as if the whole school had come out to cheer on the team.

Malik threw a few warm-up pitches and then the umpire yelled, "Play ball!"

The first Buffaloes batter stepped up to the plate.

Malik wound up and threw a fastball. The batter swung and popped the ball up. It drifted out to left field.

"I've got it," Abel called. He caught it easily and tossed the ball back to the infield.

One out, Jayden thought. He couldn't wait for his chance at bat. And hopefully for his chance to steal a base.

Malik struck out the next batter in three pitches. For the third pitch, he threw a slider that looked like it was going to be over the plate. By the time the batter swung, the ball was way out of the strike zone.

Two outs. Jayden's heart raced.

The next batter hit a line drive to first base. Wyatt leapt into the air and caught the ball for the third out. The crowd cheered.

The Redtails raced off the field, giving each other high fives and fist bumps.

Jayden got to the dugout, grabbed a helmet and bat, and walked out to the on-deck circle. He watched the Buffaloes pitcher warm up, getting a feel for his rhythm.

"Batter up!" the umpire called.

Jayden took a few practice swings and walked to home plate.

The pitcher wound up and threw. The pitch was a little inside, and Jayden let it go by.

"Ball one!" the umpire said.

The pitcher wound up again and fired a fastball right down the middle of the plate. Jayden squared around to bunt. He pushed the ball toward first base and sprinted down the first-base line. The ball rolled to a stop halfway to first, and none of the Buffaloes could get to it in time to throw Jayden out. He was safe at first!

Cody was next at bat. Jayden looked at Coach Anderson while Cody stepped into the batter's box. Coach Anderson wiped his right hand on his left sleeve, touched his cap, patted his stomach, then clapped his hands.

Jayden smiled when he saw Coach touch his cap. That was the sign to steal.

Jayden took a few steps away from first base and stared at the pitcher. He took one more step as the pitcher got ready to throw home.

Feel the rhythm, Jayden told himself.

He took a deep breath. The pitcher started his windup, and Jayden took off for second base. Halfway to second, Jayden heard the pitch land in the catcher's mitt with a thud.

Here comes the throw, he thought.

Jayden ran as fast as he could and dove into second base. His hand touched the base just as the second baseman tagged him on the shoulder. Jayden looked up at the umpire. The crowd went quiet.

After what seemed like forever, the umpire spread his arms wide and shouted, "Safe!"

The crowd roared. Jayden's teammates poured out of the dugout and ran to second base to congratulate him. They celebrated until the umpire sent the team back to the dugout so the game could continue.

The Redtails went on to win 5–0. After the game, the team headed to the locker room to celebrate. Jayden stayed behind in the dugout, looking out at the field.

"Am I interrupting?" Lindsey asked.

Jayden shook his head. Lindsey sat next to him on the bench.

"Congratulations," she said.

"Thanks for your help figuring out who stole the test key," Jayden said. "I couldn't have done it without you. I wonder what's going to happen to Nick, though."

"He'll be fine," she said, smiling. "I overheard Ms. Renner tell him that she'll let him make up the test next week."

"That's good," Jayden said.

"How come you're not celebrating with the team?" Lindsey asked.

"I will," Jayden said. "I just wanted to make this moment last as long as possible."

Lindsey dug in her bag and pulled out her notebook.

"Since you're not going anywhere," she said, "can I ask you a few questions?"

Jayden laughed.

Bryan Patrick Avery discovered his love of reading and writing at an early age when he received his first Bobbsey Twins Mystery. He writes picture books, chapter books, and graphic novels. His middle grade story, "The Magic Day Mystery," was published in 2020 in *Super Puzzletastic Mysteries*, an anthology from HarperCollins and the Mystery Writers of America. His debut picture book, *The Freeman Field Photograph*, was published in 2020. Bryan lives in northern California with his family.

GLOSSARY

alibi (AL-uh-bye)—an excuse for not being somewhere or doing something

composure (kuhm-POH-zher)—a calm state of mind

confront (kuhn-FRUHNT)—to face, especially in challenge

emigrate (EM-uh-grate)—to come from one country to live permanently in another country

frame (FRAYM)—to make an innocent person look guilty

journalist (JUR-nuhl-ist)—a person who gathers and reports news

recognize (REK-uhg-nyze)—to know and remember upon seeing

statistician (stat-ih-STISH-uhn)—someone who is responsible for recording a team's statistics

statistics (stuh-TIS-tiks)—science of collecting numerical facts, such as a baseball player's achievements on the field

suspect (SUHSS-pekt)—someone who may be responsible for a crime or wrongdoing

visualization (vih-zhoo-lye-ZAY-shuhn)—the forming of a mental picture

DISCUSSION QUESTIONS

1. Jayden is accused of stealing the answers to the math test and using the answers to cheat. He didn't do it, but Ms. Renner is certain he did. Have you ever been accused of doing something you didn't do? How did you handle it?

2. Lindsey dreams of being an award-winning journalist. What is your biggest dream? What can you do now that might help you achieve your dream in the future?

3. Discuss how the adults in the story handled the situation with Jayden. Do you think he was treated fairly? How might they have handled things differently?

WRITING PROMPTS

1. Imagine that Jayden is asked to give a thank-you speech after breaking the school record. Write Jayden's thank-you speech. Who would he thank, and why?

2. Nick admits that his time on the baseball team led to his struggles in Ms. Renner's class. He says he should have asked for help instead of trying to cheat. Write a scene where Nick asks someone (Ms. Renner, his parents, or another student) for help.

3. In order to rejoin the team, Jayden has to clear his name before the season ends. He stands up for himself. Write a short essay about a time you stood up for yourself.

MORE ABOUT STOLEN BASES

The distance from first base to second base on a baseball field is 90 feet. The distance from home plate to second base is 127 feet 3 ⅜ inches.

To steal a base, the runner must usually get from base to base in less than three and a half seconds in order to beat the throw.

Ned Cuthbert, an outfielder for the Philadelphia Keystones, stole the first base in a baseball game in 1865.

Rickey Henderson, who played Major League Baseball (MLB) for 25 years, holds the records for most stolen bases in a season (130) and a career (1,406). He also holds the record for getting caught stealing—335 times—in his career.

Robby Thompson holds the record for getting caught stealing the most times in one game—four times in 1986.

Eddie Collins, Otis Nixon, Eric Young, and Carl Crawford share the record for most stolen bases in a single game, with six. Eddie Collins did it twice!

In 2021, MLB tried out some new rules to increase the number of stolen base attempts in the minor leagues. For example, in the Triple-A league, the bases were made slightly larger. That means the distance players must run between bases is a bit shorter.

SOLVE ALL THE SPORTS MYSTERIES!

JAKE MADDOX · JV MYSTERIES

CHEER FEARS

JAKE MADDOX · JV MYSTERIES

OFF BASE

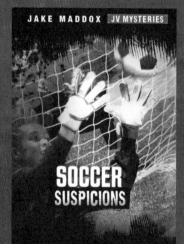

JAKE MADDOX · JV MYSTERIES

SOCCER SUSPICIONS

JAKE MADDOX · JV MYSTERIES

TRACK AND FIELD TRICK